Scardust

Dear Megan-
Always believe in
yourself and your
dreams, they do
come true! Have
a very Happy Birthday
with many more
to come!
Love + Blessings
Jennifer Devine

by **Jennifer Devine**

illustrations by Akiko K. Fry

First published by AuthorHouse 06/27/05

ISBN: 1-4208-6461-0 (sc)

Library of Congress Control Number: 2005905737

Printed in the United States of America
Bloomington, Indiana

This book is printed on acid-free paper.

Illustrations by Akiko K. Fry

authorHOUSE

1663 Liberty Drive
Bloomington, Indiana 47403
(800) 839-8640
www.authorhouse.com

This book is dedicated to God, for whom without I would not be alive; to the first people in my life who made me feel beautiful no matter what, my mother and father. Thank you to all the people who made Scardust a reality: To my husband Brian for loving me, scars and all. Akiko, for making my story come to life, to J.R. for your generous donation, Mike P. for working so hard to make this happen, and my family and friends, you know who you are.

Jenny and her daddy were driving home from the hospital where Jenny had surgery on her tummy. Jenny was looking out of the window when a ladybug landed on it.

"Look, Daddy, look!" she said pointing to the bug.

"Yeah, that's a ladybug," he said. "That's why I call you Jen-Bug, because you remind me of one."

"Why?" Jenny giggled.

Her dad winked at her through the rear-view mirror, "A ladybug means you'll have good luck," he said. "You are good luck to me."

After arriving home, Jenny was exhausted. Her mommy had her new fuzzy pink blanket that she was given by the nurses at the hospital. Mommy also gave her the tattered old pillow she had had since her first surgery, all waiting for her to snuggle up with.

Jenny sat on her favorite couch by the window, so she could look out. Jenny liked looking out at all the beautiful things, especially when she couldn't be there.

Jenny was all settled in when her daddy came to check in on her. "How's my Jen-Bug?" he asked.

Jenny's daddy noticed she was ever so carefully lifting her pajama shirt, just enough to see her new scar from her surgery.

"Try not to touch your tummy, Bug. You don't want to get germs in your new scar, or it won't heal."

Jenny looked sad. "It's kind of ugly, Daddy."

"Jen-Bug," he said, "a scar is never ugly." He paused. "You see,

God chooses very carefully who He thinks will be brave enough to handle the type of scar He gives them. That is why He makes each scar look a little different, because we are all different."

This wasn't the first time Jenny had had surgery, and this wasn't her first scar. But, this was the first time Jenny wanted to know why people have scars, and why she has scars.

"You have scars, don't you, Daddy?" she said, pointing to a scar on his arm.

"Yes, Bug, I do," he replied. "I was in an accident when I was five years old—just your age—and I have had surgery too. Some people seem to collect them as they go through life, some more than others."

"But, Daddy." Jenny paused. "Why do people have scars?"

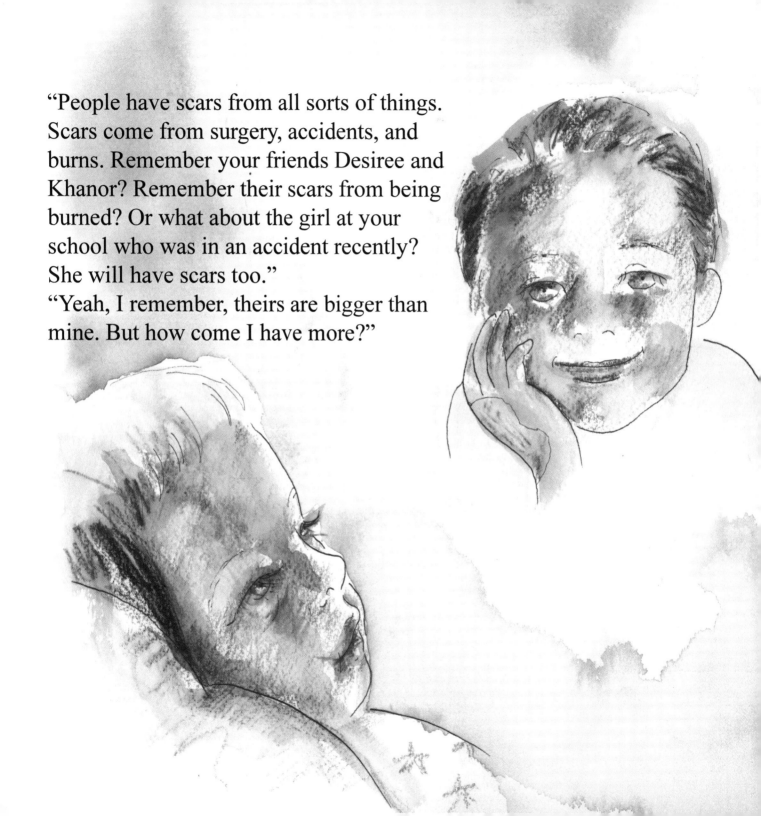

"People have scars from all sorts of things. Scars come from surgery, accidents, and burns. Remember your friends Desiree and Khanor? Remember their scars from being burned? Or what about the girl at your school who was in an accident recently? She will have scars too."

"Yeah, I remember, theirs are bigger than mine. But how come I have more?"

"You know, Bug," said her daddy, "it doesn't matter how many scars you have, or how big a scar is. Each one tells a story. We all have scars from something, whether you can see them or not. Scars come in all shapes, sizes, and even colors, just like people do."

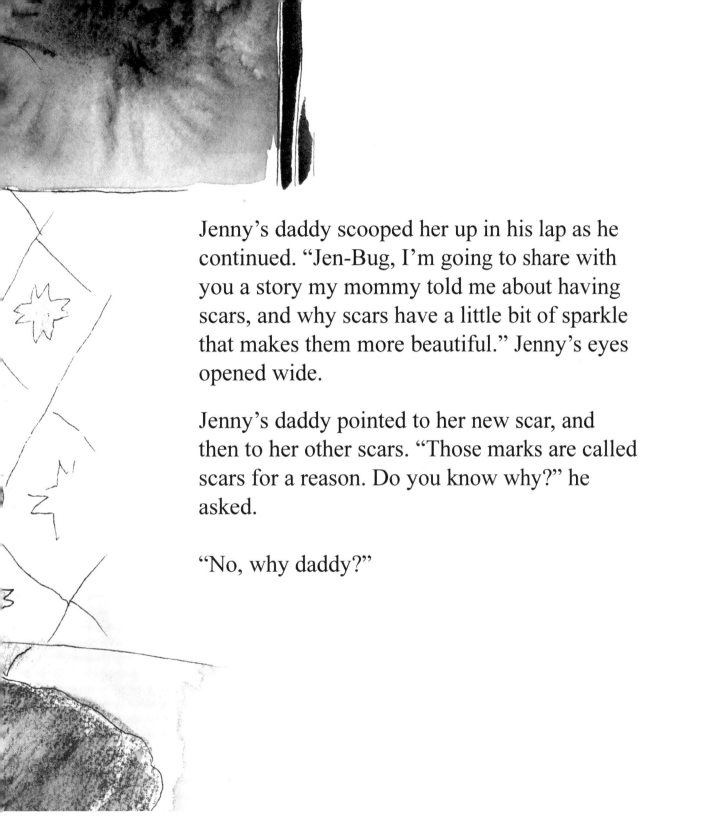

Jenny's daddy scooped her up in his lap as he continued. "Jen-Bug, I'm going to share with you a story my mommy told me about having scars, and why scars have a little bit of sparkle that makes them more beautiful." Jenny's eyes opened wide.

Jenny's daddy pointed to her new scar, and then to her other scars. "Those marks are called scars for a reason. Do you know why?" he asked.

"No, why daddy?"

He pointed to the nighttime sky. "Look at the millions of stars God has created. On one of those stars sits the Scardust Fairy."

Jenny interrupted, "Is that like the Tooth Fairy?" She began to get excited thinking how maybe now that she had her scars she would get a visit from the Scardust Fairy. It reminded her of when the Tooth Fairy visited after she lost her tooth.

"Yes, like the Tooth Fairy," he continued. "Every time you see a star fall out of the sky, the Scardust Fairy scoops up the glitter that falls behind. That glitter is called Scardust because it comes from the stars, but goes into your scars."

Jenny gasped in delight. "What does she do with it?"

"When you realize that your scars are nothing to be ashamed or embarrassed about, then the Scardust Fairy knows it is time to visit you." He continued, "One night, when you are fast asleep, the Scardust Fairy sprinkles the dust on your scars, making them even more beautiful than they already are."

"Daddy, if a scar is so beautiful, I must be really beautiful." Her daddy nodded. Jenny smiled as she felt each one of her scars.

"So why do people look at me funny when they see them?"

"Because they don't know the story of Scardust, yet." He smiled. "You are a lucky girl; you get to keep your scars for the rest of your life. But, the story of Scardust is something you can share with others like you. They, too, have had to accept the scars God has given them. You will always have a little bit of Scardust in each and every scar.

As Jenny's daddy tucked her into bed, like he did every night, he said, "Tuck you in like a bug in a rug." And, as always, this made her giggle.

He kissed her goodnight. "Love you, bug," he said. "Don't forget to say your prayers."

"Love you, Daddy," she whispered.

As he left her room, he turned back and said, "You know, your mommy and I end every night with our prayers, too. Tonight, we'll thank God for making you so special to Him that he let His very own stars become your scars."

To Parents and Professionals

When a child has a scar, or scars, and they look into the mirror, do they see the "ugliness" of their scar, or do they see the beauty and strength behind the experience that put it there?

Scars are physical marks that society has helped to make emotional insecurities. We must help our children to be sensitive and considerate to themselves and others that have physical markings, to help them understand and see the beauty behind the experiences that create the people we are today, and will become tomorrow. We can help people feel beautiful despite the scars that they perceive as making them "ugly."

It is my dream that this book can be a way of communicating to your child that can open their hearts and minds to seeing the good in all experiences, traumatic and joyful. I encourage you to help your child actively seek another person with a scar, and have them pass on the story of Scardust, as my father did to me. This will give your child an interactive way to help another person with the pain and adaptation of their scar and the experience that created it.

I am 29 years old with many, many scars from a lifetime battle with Cystic Fibrosis, a lethal, genetic disease affecting the lungs and pancreas. I am the Jenny in this story. I have had dozens of surgeries, procedures, and treatments which have built a "map of scars," showcasing every battle I have fought and overcome. I still experience daily society's intolerable cruelty to the physical display of my scars. Challenging, as it may be to feel beautiful in a world that finds ways to prevent that feeling, it is up to us to change that way of thinking. At the very least, reduce the cruelty through acceptance and understanding. I hope, very much, that "Scardust" can be a beginning of this journey for you or your child.

When I feel insecure about my scars, I always remember something I once heard, "God doesn't make mistakes, only people do."

I wish you great health and healing in your journey of life.

Sincerely,

Jennifer A. Devine

Printed in the United States
67105LVS00002B